ALIEN
INVASIONS

ALIEN INVASIONS

written and illustrated by
BENJAMIN KENDALL

LANDMARK EDITIONS, INC.
P.O. Box 4469 • 1402 Kansas Avenue • Kansas City, Missouri 64127

Dedicated to
my family and
all Aliens from outer space.

Second Printing

COPYRIGHT © 1993 BENJAMIN KENDALL

International Standard Book Number: 0-933849-42-7 (LIB.BDG.)

Library of Congress Cataloging-in-Publication Data
Kendall, Benjamin, 1984-
    Alien invasions / written and illustrated by Benjamin Kendall.
    p.   cm.
    Summary: When nine-year-old Ben discovers that his super-hero cos-
tume allows him to see the space Aliens encroaching upon his house and
school, he takes bold action against them, sometimes with humorous results.
ISBN 0-933849-42-7 (lib.bdg. : acid-free paper)
  1. Children's writings, American.
  [1. Extraterrestrial beings—Fiction.   2. Heroes—Fiction.
  3. Humorous stories.   4. Children's writings.
  5. Children's art.]
  I. Title.
PZ7.K325A1   1993
[E]—dc20   93-13423
                      2 2074   CIP
                     12-94   AC

E
K

Editorial Coordinator: Nancy R. Thatch
Creative Coordinator: David Melton

Printed in the United States of America

Landmark Editions, Inc.
P.O. Box 4469
1402 Kansas Avenue
Kansas City, Missouri 64127
(816) 241-4919

ALIEN INVASIONS

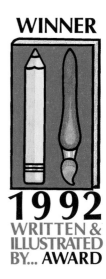

WINNER

1992
WRITTEN &
ILLUSTRATED
BY... AWARD

When I first read the opening pages of Benjamin Kendall's contest entry, ALIEN INVASIONS, I started chuckling, and I didn't stop laughing until the very last page. I hadn't had so much fun since I read James Thurber's *The Secret Life of Walter Mitty.*

In fact, Benjamin's sly approach to humor reminds me of Thurber's. Like Thurber, Benjamin never hits readers over their heads with blockbuster jokes. Instead, he gently nudges our funny bones with the clever turn of a phrase or twist of a thought. He is able to write high style comedy, and he knows how to develop illustrations that become perfect extensions of his text.

Benjamin's illustrations are not drawn in a broad cartoon style; they are composed in a rather straightforward manner. When viewed without the accompanying text, his illustrations do not appear to be whimsical. But after reading the words on the pages, one realizes how funny his pictures are. As you read ALIEN INVASIONS and look at the illustrations, you'll see exactly what I mean.

When Benjamin came to our offices, we found him to be a very quiet little boy who didn't talk much. But when he did talk, we listened carefully to what he had to say. And we discovered by the things he said that he had many ideas, terrific insights and, of course, that wonderful sense of humor which makes ALIEN INVASIONS such a delightful book.

So get ready to smile and chuckle a lot. The fun begins on the following page.

— David Melton
Creative Coordinator
Landmark Editions, Inc.

Two weeks before Halloween, I saw a terrific ad in the newspaper. It read:

This Halloween Buy A Super-Hero Costume!

It Will Protect You And Your Family

From Alien Invaders!

Fits All 9-Year-Old Boys Named Ben.

"What luck!" I thought. "The costume is just my size. I am a boy. I am nine years old. And — you guessed it — my name is Ben!"

I just had to have that super-hero costume!

When I showed the ad to my mom, she liked the costume too. So she wrote a check right then and put the order in the mail.

On Halloween morning my package finally arrived.

Boy, was I happy!

I hurried to my room and opened the box. Inside was my new super-hero costume! When I tried it on, it fit me perfectly. I proudly swirled the bright red cape around my shoulders and put on my black mask.

My super-hero costume really looked great on me! I stood before the mirror and flexed my muscles. I could feel the costume's super powers surge through my body.

I knew my exciting adventures were about to begin, but...

Mom said I had to eat ALL of my dinner before I could go trick-or-treating that night. She had cooked stuffed green peppers. Yuck! I hate stuffed peppers!

To make matters worse, I saw two Aliens sneak into our kitchen. They poured something terrible all over the peppers.

I tried to warn Mom about this, but she said she couldn't see any Aliens. And she wouldn't believe me when I told her my super-hero costume had given me super eyesight. So, I had to sit there and eat every bite of that stuffed green pepper.

When I went trick-or-treating, I found my super-hero costume made me run faster. I zoomed from house to house and got more candy than any of my friends.

After I went to bed that night, I was sick four times. I was sick in the bedroom, sick in the bathroom, and sick in the hallway — twice.

Mom said it was because I had eaten too much candy. But I knew better. I knew I was sick because of the awful stuff the Aliens had poured over the peppers!

The following morning I felt better. So I went outside to play. Mom let me wear my super-hero costume. It was a good thing, too, because there were Aliens in our trees. And they were throwing down little brown Alien eggs that looked a lot like acorns.

I quickly raked up the eggs before they had time to hatch. Because I was wearing my super-hero costume, I could rake faster than the Aliens could throw eggs. So they finally gave up.

On Monday I went to school. I took my super-hero costume for *Show and Tell*. Everyone thought my outfit was really neat.

It's a good thing I had my costume with me. During math two Aliens came into our classroom. They looked like our principal and the school librarian. But I knew better.

When I put on my super-hero costume, the Aliens hurried out of the room. I knew they were afraid of my super powers. Just before recess, I'm sure I heard their Alien spaceship blast off.

On Tuesday I wore my super-hero costume to breakfast. It was a good thing too. Aliens had taken over Mom and Dad and were controlling their minds.

Although my parents looked like they always did, they were acting very strangely. This morning they were gulping down their food really fast.

Dad said, "I'm going to be late for work!"

And Mom said, "I must rush to a special meeting!"

Well, they didn't fool me. I knew my parents had plenty of time. I knew they were really speaking to each other in Alien codes.

When I noticed Dad's briefcase in the living room, I got suspicious. I knew Aliens carried powerful mind-control machines in black briefcases.

I opened the briefcase and saw a brown paper bag. I knew an Alien machine was inside the bag, because it smelled exactly like tuna fish.

So using my super powers, I threw the bag on the floor and stomped on it. After it was smashed flat, I put it back in the case and snapped the lid shut.

Right after that, I saw Dad kiss Mom. I knew they were back to normal because Aliens don't know how to kiss.

When Dad got home that night, he was very upset.

"What's the matter?" Mom asked.

"Someone smashed my tuna fish sandwich!" he grumbled.

"Who would have done such a terrible thing?" Mom wondered.

I didn't say a word. I couldn't tell Mom and Dad how I had saved them from the Aliens. We super heroes never brag about our super powers. We try to keep them secret.

On Wednesday the Aliens did not come to our school. I thought they probably had gone back to their own planet. GOOD!

But just to be safe, I wore my super-hero costume while I played in the park that afternoon. It was a good thing, too, because I found a very strange shape on the ground.

It looked like home plate on a baseball field. But I knew better. I knew it was the exact shape an Alien spaceship would make!

But where were these Aliens hiding? I wondered. When I looked up, I saw hundreds of spaceships were parked in the trees. The Aliens had camouflaged their ships with leaves, but I could still see them.

I could see the Aliens too. They were watching me and planning how to take me prisoner. But they didn't have a chance — not with me wearing my super-hero costume. They knew my super powers could melt them into dust. I picked up a clump of dirt and crumbled it, just to let the Aliens see how powerful I really was.

On Thursday morning our real teacher was not at school. The substitute teacher, who called herself Ms. Wilson, came to our classroom. She smiled and acted like a friendly person. But I knew better. I knew Ms. Wilson was really an Alien in disguise. And I could tell the six red pencils on her desk were not pencils at all. They were really her supersonic ray guns.

When the Alien-teacher turned toward the blackboard, I grabbed her ray guns and hid them in the closet. She looked everywhere for them, but couldn't find them.

"Does anyone know where my pencils are?" she asked.

"No, Ms. Wilson," everyone replied.

I couldn't help but giggle a little.

The next morning our real teacher, Ms. Carter, returned. I took the ray guns out of the closet and gave them to her. She smiled and thanked me.

Of course, she acted like they were only pencils. But she didn't fool me. I could tell Ms. Carter knew they were really dangerous Alien weapons. I saw how carefully she placed the ray guns in her desk and locked the drawer.

That afternoon I noticed the drawer was open again and the ray guns were gone. I was sure Ms. Carter had destroyed all of them during lunch.

19

On Friday I discovered the most amazing thing about my super-hero costume. When I put on my mask upside down, I became invisible. It's true. No one could see me.

Let me tell you something — being invisible is a lot of fun. I could tickle other kids without getting punched in the nose. I could hold up a pencil and make it look like it was floating in space. I could stand next to people and listen while they told each other secrets. And I could go to a movie without buying a ticket. (But, I did that only once.)

I loved to ride my bicycle when I was invisible. It was hilarious to see how people turned and stared.

If you don't believe I was invisible, just take a look at this picture.

Can you see the bicycle whizzing along on the sidewalk?

Yes, you can!

Can you see me on the bicycle?

No, you can't!

You can't see me on the bicycle because I am INVISIBLE!

I began wearing my super-hero costume most of the time. And I saw Aliens almost everywhere I went!

When Mom and I were at the shopping mall, I saw an Alien step onto the escalator. I quickly ran over and pushed the emergency STOP button.

I had no idea the escalator would stop so fast. The Alien was hurled high into the air, and three shoppers were thrown into the water fountain.

My mom made me hurry outside before the shoppers had time to thank me.

When we were at the supermarket, Mom told me she needed some oranges. Before I could get any, an Alien appeared and knocked down the whole stack. Oranges rolled everywhere!

The manager came running. Squash! Squish! Squish! He slipped on the oranges and fell down. I could tell that he was very angry. So I didn't try to explain anything to him. I just turned my mask upside down and became invisible.

When we got home, I found a black thing on our driveway. It looked like our garage-door opener. But I knew better. I knew it was an Alien transmitter. The Aliens used it to send messages to their planet about my super-hero powers. I had to stop that!

So I opened the transmitter and yanked out two of its wires. What a mess! All the garage doors in our neighborhood started going up and down, and up and down. The doors didn't stop until I dug a hole in our back yard and buried the black thing.

Then the time I had been dreading arrived.

One evening Mom came into my room and said, "It's been two weeks since Halloween. It's time to box up your super-hero costume and put it in the attic."

"I have to get rid of the Aliens first," I told her. "So please let me keep my costume out one more day."

"Okay, one more day," she agreed. "But that's all."

I knew what I had to do. Tomorrow I would have to face the Aliens alone. The future of the world depended on me.

The next morning I put on my super-hero costume for the last time. I stood tall and proud, ready to meet the enemy. But just in case something went wrong, I said good-bye to my hamster. Then I walked down the stairs.

"Where are you going?" Mom asked.

"To the park to save the world," I announced.

"That's a good idea," she said, "but be sure you're back in time for lunch."

"I will try my best," I replied.

In spite of the dangers I faced, I walked bravely to the center of the park and stopped.

"ZIPPA, ZAPPA, ZOO!" I shouted.

In Alien language that means, "Come out, come out, wherever you are!"

The Aliens heard me. Their Leader stepped out from behind a tree. He raised his ray gun and aimed it at me.

"Only weaklings and cowards point guns at people!" I told him.

Then I stared at his ray gun with my super-laser vision. Streaks of red light shot from my eyes and melted his weapon.

The Alien Leader didn't like that one bit. The eyes on the top of his head went flipperty flop, flipperty flop. And he got a real mean look on his face.

That was his mistake! We super heroes won't stand for mean looks on Alien faces. I stepped forward, picked him up, and threw him into his spaceship.

"Leave in peace or leave in pieces!" I warned him.

The Alien Leader didn't have to be told twice. He slammed the spaceship door shut, started his rockets, and blasted off into outer space. The other Aliens fired up their rockets too. Then off they went in their spaceships — Zoom! Zoom! Zoom! And they were GONE!

When I looked at my wrist watch, I was pleased. I could be home in time for lunch. We super heroes always try to be on time.

That evening I folded my super-hero costume and placed it neatly in its box. As I put the box on a shelf in the attic, I was surprised to find something else — another costume box. I quickly opened it, and guess what I found inside? It was an astronaut suit, complete with helmet and a six-rocket backpack.

"Just what I need!" I exclaimed. "Next week I can save Mars!"

BOOKS FOR STUDENTS

— WINNERS OF THE NATIONAL WRITTEN

by Benjamin Kendall, age 7
State College, Pennsylvania

When Ben wears his new super-hero costume, he sees Aliens who are from outer space. His attempts to stop the pesky invaders provide loads of laughs. Colorful drawings add to the fun!

Printed Full Color
ISBN 0-933849-42-7

by Steven Shepard, age 13
Great Falls, Virginia

A gripping thriller! When a boy rows his boat to an island to retrieve a stolen knife, he faces threatening fog, treacherous currents, and a sinister lobsterman. Outstanding drawings!

Printed Full Color
ISBN 0-933849-43-5

by Travis Williams, age 16
Sardis, B.C., Canada

A chilling mystery! When a teen-age boy discovers his classmates are missing, he becomes entrapped in a web of conflicting stories, false alibis, and frightening changes. Dramatic drawings!

Printed Two Colors
ISBN 0-933849-44-3

by Dubravka Kolanović, age 18
Savannah, Georgia

Ivan enjoys a wonderful day with his grandparents, a dog, a cat, and a delightful bear that is *always* hungry. Cleverly written, brilliantly illustrated! Little kids love this book!

Printed Full Color
ISBN 0-933849-45-1

by Amy Jones, age 17
Shirley, Arkansas

A whirlwind adventure! An encha unicorn helps a young girl rescue eccentric aunt from the evil Sulta Zabar. A charming story. Lovely trations add a magical glow!

Printed Full Color
ISBN 0-933849-46-X

by Cara Reichel, age 15
Rome, Georgia

Elegant and eloquent! A young stonecutter vows to create a great statue for his impoverished village. But his fame almost stops him from fulfilling that promise.

Printed Two Colors
ISBN 0-933849-35-4

by Jonathan Kahn, age 9
Richmond Heights, Ohio

A fascinating nature story! While Patulous, a prairie rattlesnake, searches for food, he must try to avoid the claws and fangs of his own enemies.

Printed Full Color
ISBN 0-933849-36-2

by Jayna Miller, age 19
Zanesville, Ohio

The funniest Halloween ever! When Jammer the Rabbit takes all the treats, his friends get even. Their hilarious scheme includes a haunted house and mounds of chocolate.

Printed Full Color
ISBN 0-933849-37-0

by Lauren Peters, age 7
Kansas City, Missouri

The Christmas that almost wasn't! When Santa Claus takes a vacation, Mrs. Claus and the elves go on strike. Toys aren't made. Cookies aren't baked. Super illustrations.

Printed Full Color
ISBN 0-933849-25-7

by Michael Cain, age 11
Annapolis, Maryland

A glorious tale of adventure become a knight, a young man face a beast in the forest, a s binding witch, and a giant bird guards a magic oval crystal.

Printed Full Color
ISBN 0-933849-26-5

by Heidi Salter, age 19
Berkeley, California

Spooky and wonderful! To save her vivid imagination, a young girl must confront the Great Grey Grimly himself. The narrative is filled with suspense. Vibrant illustrations.

Printed Full Color
ISBN 0-933849-21-4

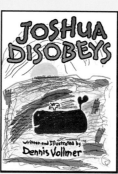

by Dennis Vollmer, age 6
Grove, Oklahoma

A baby whale's curiosity gets him into a lot of trouble. GUINNESS BOOK OF RECORDS lists Dennis as the youngest author/illustrator of a published book.

Printed Full Color
ISBN 0-933849-12-5

by Lisa Gross, age 12
Santa Fe, New Mexico

A touching story of self-esteem! A puppy is laughed at because of his unusual appearance. His search for acceptance is told with sensitivity and humor. Wonderful illustrations.

Printed Full Color
ISBN 0-933849-13-3

by Stacy Chbosky, age 14
Pittsburgh, Pennsylvania

A powerful plea for freedom! This emotion-packed story of a young slave touches an essential part of the human spirit. Made into a film by Disney Educational Productions.

Printed Full Color
ISBN 0-933849-14-1

by Amy Hagstrom, age 9
Portola, California

An exciting western! When a and an old Indian try to save a h of wild ponies, they discover a canyon and see the mystical vis of the Great White Stallion.

Printed Full Color
ISBN 0-933849-15-X

Winning THE NATIONAL WRITTEN & ILLUSTRATED BY... AWARDS CONTEST was one of the most important events in my life! I'm very grateful to Landmark Editions for launching my career. The opportunities they gave me and continue to give to other young author/illustrators are invaluable.

—Dav Pilkey, author/illustrator
WORLD WAR WON
and 12 other published books

Share these wonderful books with your students and watch their imaginations soar!

As Rhonda Freese, Teacher, writes:
After I showed the Winning Books to my students, all they wanted to do was WRITE! WRITE! WRITE! and DRAW! DRAW! DRAW!

To motivate and inspire your students, order the Award-Winning Books today! Make sure your students experience all of these important books.

...nnie-Alise Leggat, age 8
...oeper, Virginia

...Kendrick wants to play foot-
...but her mother wants her to
...ne a ballerina. Their clash of
...creates hilarious situations.
...r, delightful illustrations.

...d Full Color
...0-933849-39-7

by Lisa Kirsten Butenhoff, age 13
Woodbury, Minnesota

The people of a Russian village face
the winter without warm clothes or
enough food. Then their lives are
improved by a young girl's gifts. A
tender story with lovely illustrations.

Printed Full Color
ISBN 0-933849-40-0

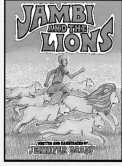

by Jennifer Brady, age 17
Columbia, Missouri

When poachers capture a pride of
lions, a native boy tries to free
the animals. A skillfully told story.
Glowing illustrations illuminate this
African adventure.

Printed Full Color
ISBN 0-933849-41-9

by Aruna Chandrasekhar, age 9
Houston, Texas

A touching and timely story! When
the lives of many otters are threat-
ened by a huge oil spill, a group of
concerned people come to their
rescue. Wonderful illustrations.

Printed Full Color
ISBN 0-933849-33-8

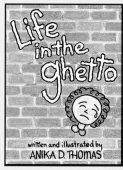

by Anika D. Thomas, age 13
Pittsburgh, Pennsylvania

A compelling autobiography! A
young girl's heartrending account
of growing up in a tough, inner-city
neighborhood. The illustrations
match the mood of this gripping story.

Printed Two Colors
ISBN 0-933849-34-6

...ity Gaige, age 16
...ading, Pennsylvania

...cal blend of poetry and pho-
...phs! Amity's sensitive poems
...thought-provoking ideas and
...ng insights. This lovely book
...to be savored and enjoyed.

...d Full Color
...0-933849-27-3

by Adam Moore, age 9
Broken Arrow, Oklahoma

A remarkable true story! When Adam
was eight years old, he fell and ran
an arrow into his head. With rare
insight and humor, he tells of his
ordeal and his amazing recovery.

Printed Two Colors
ISBN 0-933849-24-9

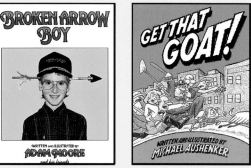

by Michael Aushenker, age 19
Ithaca, New York

Chomp! Chomp! When Arthur for-
gets to feed his goat, the animal eats
everything in sight. A very funny
story — good to the last bite. The
illustrations are terrific.

Printed Full Color
ISBN 0-933849-28-1

by Leslie Ann MacKeen, age 9
Winston-Salem, North Carolina

Loaded with fun and puns! When
Jeremiah T. Fitz's car stops running,
several animals offer suggestions for
fixing it. The results are hilarious.
The illustrations are charming.

Printed Full Color
ISBN 0-933849-19-2

by Elizabeth Haidle, age 13
Beaverton, Oregon

A very touching story! The grump-
iest Elfkin learns to cherish the
friendship of others after he helps
an injured snail and befriends an
orphaned boy. Absolutely beautiful.

Printed Full Color
ISBN 0-933849-20-6

...aac Whitlatch, age 11
...sper, Wyoming

...rue confessions of a devout
...able hater! Isaac tells ways to
...and dispose of the "slimy green
...s." His colorful illustrations
...de a salad of laughter and mirth.

...d Full Color
...-933849-16-8

by Dav Pilkey, age 19
Cleveland, Ohio

A thought-provoking parable! Two
kings halt an arms race and learn to
live in peace. This outstanding book
launched Dav's professional career. He
now has had many books published.

Printed Full Color
ISBN 0-933849-22-2

by David McAdoo, age 14
Springfield, Missouri

An exciting intergalactic adventure!
In the distant future, a courageous
warrior defends a kingdom from a
dragon from outer space. Astound-
ing sepia illustrations.

Printed Duotone
ISBN 0-933849-23-0

by Karen Kerber, age 12
St. Louis, Missouri

A delightfully playful book! The text
is loaded with clever alliterations and
gentle humor. Karen's brightly col-
ored illustrations are composed of
wiggly and waggly strokes of genius.

Printed Full Color
ISBN 0-933849-29-X

**THIS SPACE
IS
RESERVED
FOR A
WONDERFUL
NEW BOOK**

written &
illustrated by
ONE OF YOUR
STUDENTS

The Landmark books are so popular in our school that I had to
place them on a special shelf in our library. Now that shelf is
always empty.
—Jean Kern, Library Media Specialist

..These books will inspire young writers because of the quality of
the works, as well as the young ages of their creators. [They] will
prove worthwhile additions for promoting values discussions and
encouraging creative writing. —SCHOOL LIBRARY JOURNAL

Having my book published is so exciting! It is fun to be
on TV and radio talk shows. And I loved speaking in schools
across the country. I enjoy meeting students and encouraging
them to write and illustrate their own books.

—Karen Kerber, author/illustrator
WALKING IS WILD, WEIRD & WACKY

Jayna Miller
age 19

Lauren Peters
age 7

Michael Cain
age 11

Heidi Salter
age 19

Amity Gaige
age 16

Dennis Vollmer
age 6

Lisa Gross
age 12

Stacy Chbosky
age 14

Karen Kerber
age 12

David McAdoo
age 14

THE WINNERS OF THE 1993 NATIONAL
WRITTEN & ILLUSTRATED BY... AWARDS FOR STUDENTS®

FIRST PLACE 6-9 Age Category	**FIRST PLACE** 10-13 Age Category	**FIRST PLACE** 14-19 Age Category

Shintaro Maeda, age 8 Wichita, Kansas	Miles MacGregor, age 12 Phoenix, Arizona	Kristin Pedersen, age 18 Etobicoke, Ont., Canada

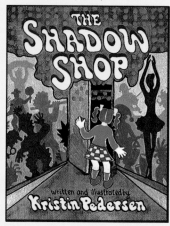

The birds will not fly in Thomas Raccoon's airshow unless Mr. Eagle approves. And everyone is afraid to talk to Mr. Eagle. So Thomas must face the big grumpy bird alone. Terrific color illustrations add exciting action to the story.

29 Pages, Full Color
ISBN 0-933849-51-6

In a dark, barren land, a young Indian boy dreams of a marvelous Sunflower that can light and warm the earth. To save his tribe from starvation, he must find the flower before it's too late. A beautifully illustrated legend.

29 Pages, Full Color
ISBN 0-933849-52-4

When Thelma McMurty trades her shadow for another one, she thinks she will live happily ever after. But an old gypsy woman knows better. Cleverly told in rhyme. The collage illustrations create a spooky, surreal atmosphere.

29 Pages, Full Color
ISBN 0-933849-53-2

BOOKS FOR STUDENTS BY STUDENTS

Written & Illustrated by...
a revolutionary two-brain approach for teaching students how to write and illustrate amazing books

David Melton

Written & Illustrated by . . .
by David Melton

This highly acclaimed teacher's manual offers classroom-proven, step-by-step instructions in all aspects of teaching students how to write, illustrate, assemble, and bind original books. Loaded with information and positive approaches that really work. Contains lesson plans, more than 200 illustrations, and suggested adaptations for use at all grade levels K through college.

The results are dazzling!
Children's Book Review Service, Inc.

WRITTEN & ILLUSTRATED BY... provides a current of enthusiasm, positive thinking and faith in the creative spirit of children. David Melton has the heart of a teacher.
THE READING TEACHER

. . .an exceptional book! Just browsing through it stimulates excitement for writing
Joyce E. Juntune, Executive Director
The National Association for Creativity

A "how to" book that really works.
Judy O'Brien, Teacher

Softcover, 96 Pages
ISBN 0-933849-00-1

LANDMARK EDITIONS, INC.
P.O. BOX 4469 • KANSAS CITY, MISSOURI 64127 • (816) 241-4919